For

Ayesha and Amaya

As wondrous as the sun, moon and stars to me…

For

Samara and Sana

Who find magic in every story.

The Kidnapping of Amir Hamza

From the Mughal Manuscript
Hamzanama

Retold by
Mamta Dalal Mangaldas
and Saker Mistri

Mapin Publishing

About the Book

The *Hamzanama* (or *The Story of Amir Hamza*) was the most popular epic during the Mughal period. Full of giants, demons, dragons, heroes and beautiful princesses, these great adventure stories were narrated around camp fires and in courts in Iran, Central Asia, India, and even across the Indian Ocean, in Indonesia.

In fact, the *Hamzanama* was one of the favourite stories of the great Mughal Emperor Akbar. In the 16th century, when the 13-year-old Emperor ascended the throne, he commissioned a grand illustration of the *Hamzanama*. It took 100 artists over 15 years to complete the illustration. The resulting manuscript included over 1400 magical paintings, which illustrated 360 tales. Today only about 200 of these paintings are known to exist.

The Kidnapping of Amir Hamza contains a retelling of one exciting tale from the *Hamzanama* and is lavishly illustrated with the original paintings that Emperor Akbar enjoyed. The chapter "Akbar's Painting Workshop" introduces children to the creation of Mughal paintings and the chapter "Ways of Seeing: Be an Art Detective" shows them different ways of seeing Mughal art.

The paintings in *The Kidnapping of Amir Hamza* belong to the MAK—Austrian Museum of Applied Arts/Contemporary Art, Vienna, the Victoria and Albert Museum, London and The Aga Khan Trust for Culture.

Contents

Introduction
Akbar and His *Hamzanama*

In 1556, a 13-year-old boy became the Emperor of India. His name was Prince Akbar. A courageous and outgoing young man, he grew to be one of the greatest of the Mughal emperors, ruling over one of the richest and most powerful kingdoms in the world.

When Akbar ascended the throne, he took charge of the Mughal armies and opposed anyone who thought he was too young, or not smart enough, to rule. His kingdom stretched from Afghanistan in the northwest to Bengal in the east and halfway down the Deccan. His grandfather Babur had been the first in his family to rule India. Akbar inherited his grandfather's fascination for the many different kinds of people who lived in India, and his passionate love for history. However, he did not inherit his grandfather's interest in reading and writing. While Babur had kept a very detailed diary of all the events at court, and written poetry too, Akbar preferred physical activities: riding horses and elephants, as well as hunting, wrestling and other sports. The important things that happened at Akbar's court were also written down, but by others, not by the Emperor himself. These records eventually became a book, the *Akbarnama (The Story of Akbar)*, showing how the young Emperor Akbar became an even more powerful ruler than either his grandfather Babur or his father, Humayun.

Akbar was an Islamic king, yet he encouraged his subjects—many of whom were Hindus—to practise whatever beliefs they wished. His curiosity was balanced by his energy. He met and talked with merchants, missionaries and other travellers who came to India, seeking to learn about them and the countries they came from.

Akbar never lost his love of adventure and he often took great risks. The painting on the facing page is from the *Akbarnama*. It shows the young prince riding his elephant. His companions had stopped at the banks of the River Ganga, which was swollen with floodwaters from the heavy monsoon rains. But Akbar, not worried about the depth or the strength of the fast-moving waters, rode his elephant across—to the amazement of his companions, one of whom was Darbar Khan, the storyteller. Listening to stories seems to have been so important to Akbar that he took his storyteller on many of his expeditions.

In Mughal times, storytellers like Darbar Khan were expected not only to recite stories perfectly from memory, but also to elaborate on favourite parts and even invent new episodes. One of the young Emperor Akbar's favourite stories was the *Hamzanama—The Story of Amir Hamza*, a Persian warrior. The *Hamzanama* was a tale popular from Iran through Central Asia and India, and even across the Indian Ocean, in Indonesia. Full of giants, demons, dragons, heroes, beautiful princesses, and people from many different countries, these were great adventure stories to hear in the evening, after the excitement of a day spent hunting elephants! Akbar had a special fondness for elephants and kept hundreds of them in the royal stables.

Soon after he became emperor, Akbar decided he wanted the *Hamzanama* stories to be written down and also illustrated. He hired painters and scribes, and men skilled in making paper and pigments, and put them to work on this mammoth task. It took 100 artists over 15 years to complete the illustration and the inscription of the *Hamzanama*. The resulting manuscript included over 1400 very large and intricately detailed paintings.

These paintings remained in the Mughal Imperial Library at the Red Fort for nearly 170 years till the Persian ruler Nadir Shah looted Delhi and took away the magnificent Peacock Throne, the largest diamond in the world—the Kohinoor, and the beautiful *Hamzanama* paintings. When one of the last rulers of the Mughal dynasty, Muhammad Shah sent a special request for the return of the *Hamzanama* paintings, Nadir Shah said, "Ask but the return of all your treasures, and they are yours—but not the *Hamzanama*!"

Over the years, several of those 1400 paintings made for Akbar were scattered across the world, and some of them certainly destroyed. Today only about 200 paintings are known to exist. The largest group of paintings is in the MAK—Austrian Museum of Applied Arts/Contemporary Art—a museum in Vienna. A number of those are reproduced in this book.

Milo C. Beach, Retired Director
Freer Gallery of Art and Arthur M. Sackler Gallery,
Smithsonian Institution, Washington, D. C.

"The next day, His Majesty Emperor Akbar sat upon that glorious throne, and graciously commanded those present to be seated. And for the purpose of cheering the heart and amusing the mind, he listened for a while to a few of Darbar Khan's stories of Amir Hamza and granted happiness among his assembly."

From the *Akbarnama—The Story of Akbar*
by Abul Fazl, Akbar's court biographer

Meet the Characters

Amir Hamza
A handsome, brave and proud Persian warrior.

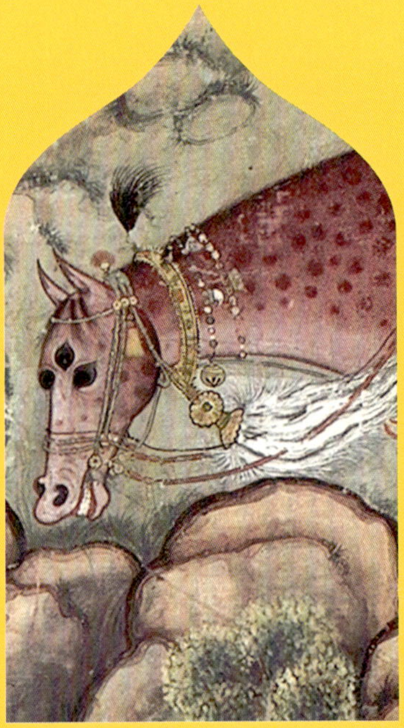

Ashqar
Hamza's three-eyed magical horse.

Ayjil
Hamza's strong brother—in a plumed turban.

Alamshah
Hamza's son—in the yellow *jama*.

Tul Mast
Hamza's large, dark-skinned companion.

Umar

Loyal friend of Hamza.

Zumurrud Shah

A cruel giant, and Hamza's enemy.

Malik Argus

The wicked and unlawful king of Takaw.

Shahrashob

Sly and mean, the disturber of the city.

Akbar and the Storyteller

Once upon a time, there lived in India a young emperor who loved to ride wild elephants. He used to roam far and wide with his soldiers, through the forests and mountains of his kingdom, crossing deep and fast-flowing rivers, in search of these mighty beasts.

One day, when the young emperor was out riding in the forests of Narwar in North India, he saw a herd of wild elephants. He chased them deep into the woods and ordered his men to use rope snares and capture the elephants. The huge legs of the elephants became entangled in the ropes and, as they struggled to free themselves, the emperor leapt on to the back of the leader of the herd. Digging his heels behind the matriarch's ears, he commanded the wild beast to be calm. Once the elephants were subdued, the emperor left his soldiers in charge, and rode back to the camp to rest in his tent.

On the evening of the elephant hunt, the sun set quietly over the forests. It did not want to disturb the Ruler of Rulers, the Badshah, the Noblest Emperor of all times: Akbar the Great. In Akbar's camp the men were bustling about, waiting for Darbar Khan, Akbar's court storyteller. The emperor loved listening to tales of magic and adventure, and took his storyteller with him wherever he went. Akbar sat in a large and resplendent tent, drumming his fingers impatiently on the rubies and diamonds on his throne.

When Darbar Khan finally entered the royal tent, Akbar leapt up to embrace him and said fondly, "Come and amuse us with one of your stories." Then he turned to his men, "Darbar Khan can tell a different story every day, for a whole year. He is a wonderful storyteller. When he describes a rainstorm, you will shiver and feel the cold wind on your face. If he portrays

a battle scene, the very ground trembles with the sound of horses and elephants in full charge."

Often the storytelling continued for many hours and was accompanied by music and dancing. As he listened with his head propped on one hand, Akbar found himself wishing he could read. It would be fun, he thought to himself, to be able to read stories on his own—but then, he wouldn't have the wonderful voice and expressive hands of Darbar Khan to transport him to these exciting new worlds.

The musicians took their places, and Darbar Khan in his scarlet robe bowed low before the emperor. "Today's tale, my Badshah, is from your favourite book: the *Hamzanama*. There is no other book like it in the whole world. The paintings in the book are so dazzling that when you see them, it is as wondrous as seeing the sun and the moon for the very first time. The colours glow like the jewels in your majesty's throne. And the hero of my story, the great Persian warrior Amir Hamza, is as strong and brave...," Darbar Khan smiled, "well, almost as strong and brave... as you, my Emperor!"

The Red Bundle

Darbar Khan opens a large box of paintings. The storyteller's young assistant holds up a painting made of stiff cotton cloth and the opener of the magic chest of stories begins his tale…

A long time ago in the land of Persia, lived a fearless nobleman called Amir Hamza. Hamza was known to fight wild animals with his bare hands and one thrust from his gleaming sword could frighten away an entire army. Hamza travelled across Persia, India and China. Everywhere he went he fought against the wicked and protected the good. He attacked the giants who troubled innocent people, overthrew evil kings, and killed fire-breathing dragons that destroyed cities.

One day, as Hamza sat in the shade of a cherry tree in his garden, watching the fountains and enjoying the cool breeze, he saw a blue rock-pigeon circling above him in the cloudless sky. His heart missed a beat: the rock-pigeon lived near the shores of the Caspian Sea and Hamza wondered why the bird had flown so far from its home. Was it carrying a message for him? The bird slowly descended and landed at the edge of a fountain very close to where Hamza sat. It looked very tired after its flight. The Amir cupped some water in his palms for the bird to drink and saw a message strapped to its leg.

The letter was from the starving farmers of Sabayil, a coastal town along the calm waters of the Caspian Sea. "Oh, Courageous Amir," it said, "we are in trouble. The heartless landlords have stolen all the crops, leaving our children hungry and crying. Please help us to fight the landlords and rescue our families from starvation." Hamza's eyes narrowed and he clenched his fist in anger at the cruel landowners. That afternoon he left for Sabayil with Ashqar, his three-eyed magical horse.

When Hamza arrived in Sabayil, he pleaded with the landlords to help the farmers who worked their land. But when Hamza asked them to share their harvest with the farmers, they laughed, "Who cares if the farmers don't eat?" Enraged, Hamza told the farmers, "Stop working in the fields of these greedy landlords. Let their fields dry up, then they too will have nothing to eat." The farmers stopped working, and soon enough, the fields became dry and hard and all the crops died. When the landlords had no food to eat, they realized that they needed the farmers to work their land and were forced to pay their wages and share the crops with them.

The people of Sabayil danced with joy. Hamza had saved their families from starvation. Their beautiful princess was so impressed by the noble Hamza that she offered him her hand in marriage. The Persian warrior accepted and soon the city was busy preparing for the royal wedding. Hamza sent word to his friends and family in Persia, asking them to come to Sabayil for the celebrations.

But not everyone was happy with Hamza's victory. The spy Shahrashob, whose very name meant "disturber of the city", was jealous of Hamza's success, and was furious that the princess wanted to marry

Hamza and not himself. He decided to get rid of Hamza. Shahrashob went to his friend Mahzub, the moneylender, and said, "If you help me to carry out my plan to kidnap Hamza and take him away to the kingdom of Takaw, I will give you a sack of gold coins." Mahzub greedily licked his lips and quickly agreed.

For many days, Shahrashob and Mahzub secretly followed Hamza. One day they saw Hamza riding Ashqar near the seashore. The Amir was alone and unarmed. Shahrashob and Mahzub had been waiting for this opportunity. The cowards hid behind a bush and when Hamza rode past, they leapt on him from behind. They pulled him off his horse and tied him up with heavy chains. The chains weighed 11,000 kilogrammes. Hamza struggled to free himself. But he fought in vain. Shahrashob and Mahzub threw a large red cloth around Hamza and dragged him, kicking and shouting, down to the water and into a boat.

Shahrashob quickly jumped into the boat and waved goodbye to Mahzub. He sat beside the red bundle in which Hamza was trapped, ready for the difficult journey to Takaw. The sailors rowed with all their strength against the waves that crashed into their boat. Mahzub stood on the shore watching the boat become smaller and smaller as it sailed away, until he could see only the dark waves swirling in the sea.

Ashqar, Hamza's faithful horse, stood near the large rocks at the water's edge and watched helplessly as his master was taken away. Ashqar was no ordinary horse; his mother was a fairy and his father a demon. Ashqar had three eyes, one of which was in the middle of his forehead. He had splendid wings and a shiny crimson coat. Ashqar's bridle and saddle were woven from gold and he wore a golden bell around his neck. The bell tinkled as he sadly shook his head from side to side. Even Ashqar, with all his magical powers, knew it would take a miracle to rescue his beloved master.

Umar Sets Sail

The master weaver of fantastic tales takes out another painting and points to Hamza's friend Umar, standing in a magnificent boat with blue and gold sails.

Amir Hamza's best and most loyal friend was Umar. Together, Umar and Hamza had sailed across rough seas, and walked through thick jungles in search of Hamza's enemies who were creating trouble in the world. When Umar received the message that Hamza was to be married in Sabayil, he was thrilled and immediately set off to join his friend for the wedding celebrations.

When he arrived in Sabayil, Umar was eager to meet Hamza and his lovely princess. He had not seen Hamza for many months and was looking forward to seeing him and exchanging stories But strangely, no one seemed to know where Hamza was. Umar looked everywhere, feeling more and more uneasy when he could not find his friend. His worry turned to alarm when he came upon Ashqar wandering alone by the seashore. Ashqar's large eyes looked sad and

he lowered his head. As Umar stroked Ashqar's silken mane, he wondered aloud: "Hamza never leaves his horse all alone like this. Where could he be?"

Umar wasted no time. He ran to the city square and called a meeting. He stood in the middle of the street and shouted, "Has anyone seen my Lord, Amir Hamza?" The people of Sabayil knew what had happened but were frightened to tell Umar the truth. Shahrashob and Mahzub the moneylender were powerful men and had threatened to kill anyone who talked about the Amir's disappearance. Umar was faced with a stony silence. He questioned the people, but no one said a word.

Suddenly, from the corner of his eye, he saw someone trying to slink away from the edge of the crowd. Umar leapt upon the man and grabbed him by his collar, "Who are you and why are you running away?" he demanded. "Do you know where Hamza is?" The man turned pale and stuttered, "I am Mahzub the moneylender. I know

nothing. I am innocent." Umar threatened Mahzub: "If you are crooked, you will go to hell. If you are truthful, I will forgive you." But Mahzub kept shaking his head and refused to speak. Umar became suspicious, "Arrest this man!" he commanded. "Seal his house and bring all his slaves to the square."

The slaves huddled together in front of Umar, too frightened to speak. Finally, one brave slave whispered, "I know where Hamza is. My master Mahzub, and Shahrashob the spy bundled up the Amir in a large red sack and threw him into a boat. They have sailed towards Takaw in the East." Umar was furious. His eyes blazed with anger and he ordered his men, "Hang Mahzub, and give his wealth to the slave who had the courage to tell me the truth."

In great haste, Umar prepared to set sail to rescue his friend. The noblemen of the city gathered a fearless crew to accompany Umar and lent him weapons to fight the pirates he might meet on the high seas. They prayed for Hamza to return safely to Sabayil and marry their beautiful princess.

When it was time to set sail, Umar stood in his boat and thanked his friends and patrons who came to say goodbye. The strong winds filled the sails and the fish jumped in and out of the rough waters. And Umar began his search for Hamza.

A Room in the Caravanserai

Darbar Khan, the magician, pulls out new heroes from his magic box of stories.

Hamza's brother Ayjil, his son Alamshah and their friend Tul Mast were also on their way to Sabayil for Hamza's wedding. After many days at sea, they ran into a heavy storm. The waves rose high, dark clouds covered the moon and stars, and they were blown off course by the strong winds.

One night, their boat finally ran aground, on a sandy beach barely lit by a pale moon. The three companions overheard some sailors talking in a strange language. Under the cover of darkness, they quickly heaved the boat ashore and hid it under a mound of sand. When they walked into the town, they realized to their horror that they were in Takaw, the kingdom of Hamza's enemy, Malik Argus. They knew that if they were discovered, Malik Argus would surely kill them. So, they traded their Persian clothes and disguised themselves as local merchants and went in search of a room. They knocked on the doors of several inns in town, but all of them were full. Finally, their boatman took them to an innkeeper who gave them a room in his caravanserai.

The caravanserai was a noisy place filled with travellers, merchants and animals. Camels chewed hay, grinding their teeth as their jaws moved from side to side. Tired soldiers put aside their weapons and lay down to rest. The three men were led through a dim doorway, up a narrow staircase, to a tiny room on the upper floor of the caravanserai. It was small and cramped but it was the only vacant room.

Hamza's friends now had a place to sleep but no money to buy food. The innkeeper was a kind man. "I will help you," he told them. "I know a merchant I can trust and he will exchange your gold belts and jewelled daggers for money."

"Do you see them?" asks Darbar Khan. "Look! They are easy to recognize: Tul Mast is large and dark-skinned, Ayjil's red turban has a crimson feather and Hamza's son, Alamshah, is wearing a yellow *jama*."

In a short while the merchant arrived, and by a stroke of luck, he turned out to be an old friend of Alamshah and Hamza. In hushed voices, the precious weapons and belts were exchanged for money. The merchant also had some important news for them. He had heard rumours that Hamza had been kidnapped from Sabayil, and was on his way to Takaw. "If Hamza is in danger, I will help you to rescue him," the merchant promised. "The people of Takaw hate Malik Argus. He has brought them nothing but misery." Ayjil, Alamshah and Tul Mast could not sleep that night. They were worried about Hamza.

The next day while they were resting in their room, there was a roll of drums in the street below. They ran to the window and heard a royal messenger make an announcement: "Tomorrow all the men of the kingdom must gather in the palace gardens. There will be a competition to choose the strongest man in Takaw. The winner will get a bag of gold coins."

There was a lot of excitement in the city as many men prepared for the competition. Each one was eager to win the prize. Hamza's friends did not know whether they should go to the contest. They knew that it could be very dangerous and that they would be killed if they were recognized. But the next morning when the sun lit the world, the three Persians decided to take a chance and go along to see the competition. They wanted to see if the men of Takaw were as strong as the Persians. Dressed as local merchants, Ayjil, Alamshah and Tul Mast joined the crowd making its way towards the palace gardens.

The painting of the caravanserai is carefully put away in a wooden box and Akbar and his men wait eagerly to see the next picture and hear more of the story.

The Contest

Emperor Akbar looks in awe at the painting of the splendid palace garden that is held up before him, as the storyteller, painter of ideas, draws another picture in the minds of his audience.

Malik Argus had the most splendid garden in the world. It was paradise. Rose buds and pomegranates shining like rubies, decorated the bushes. The pebbles in the stream sparkled like turquoise jewels. The flowers smelled so sweet, that when a breeze ruffled their petals, the whole city was perfumed. In a corner of this garden stood a majestic *chinar* tree, blazing with copper and amber-coloured leaves. The tree looked as if it was on fire.

The people of Takaw thronged to the royal garden. The air was full of excitement as the palace drums rolled and the trumpets blared. Two arrow-shots away, a pavilion had been erected for the King Malik Argus and his guest, the giant Zumurrud Shah. Everyone took their places. The contest was about to begin.

The past champion, Mahlaj Khan, galloped into the garden on his handsome horse and boasted, "I can lift the heaviest weights in the world. Let me prove my strength. I will win again this year!"

A camel strapped with heavy sand bags on its back was brought before him. The champion stabbed the camel with a long spear.

The spear went right through the animal and came out on the other side. Then he lifted the camel with one arm and tossed it over his shoulder. As the poor camel groaned in pain and died, Mahlaj Khan lifted his arms in victory.

For the second part of the contest, Mahlaj Khan charged on his horse and plunged his spear into the huge trunk of the *chinar* tree. Like a bolt of lightning, the spear split the massive tree in two and remained firmly embedded in the trunk. Zumurrud Shah put his finger on his lips, amazed at this show of strength.

The crowds cheered as King Argus, in a bright yellow *jama*, showered Mahlaj Khan with money. The coins fell all around Mahlaj Khan, like golden rain.

Mahlaj Khan proudly threw back his head and challenged, "I dare any man to pull out my spear!" A hush fell over the crowd and everyone wondered, "Who will meet this challenge? Will it be the king of Takaw, or the giant Zumurrud Shah?" But neither the king nor the giant came forward. It was Ayjil, Hamza's brother, who stepped out of the crowd. Mahlaj Khan sneered. How could this weakling do better than the mighty Mahlaj? Ayjil grabbed the spear and pulled it out of the tree in one effortless stroke. Then, with all his might, he thrust the spear into an enormous rock at the foot of the tree. As the rock shattered, sparks flew from the spear like fireworks. The crowds stood up and applauded. It was clear that Ayjil was the winner!

Malik Argus walked into the garden to give Ayjil a bag of gold coins. But as he came closer, his eyes narrowed. Surely it looked like... it could not be... but it was—Hamza's brother! For a moment he stood as still as a statue and then his face grew red with anger. "Arrest that man!" he ordered, and in a flash, Ayjil was surrounded by soldiers. "Throw him into prison," growled Zumurrud Shah. But the cowardly Malik Argus whispered to Zumurrud Shah, "Hamza is a powerful warrior and if we capture his brother, his army will certainly attack us. Let's just ask him to leave." Zumurrud Shah nodded and Malik Argus told his soldiers to remove Ayjil from his royal garden.

Ayjil together with Alamshah and Tul Mast quickly walked back to the safety of the caravanserai, before the king changed his mind and arrested him.

Shahrashob Arrives in Takaw

Darbar Khan points to a new painting and says, "What troubled times! Even a sea monster has emerged from the depths of the inky ocean to see the great Amir bound in chains."

After a long and uncomfortable journey, Shahrashob's boats finally reached the shores of Takaw. Shahrashob proudly stepped ashore to greet Malik Argus, the King of Takaw. He had captured the great warrior Amir Hamza and he was expecting to be handsomely rewarded.

It was a sunny day in Takaw and the trees and flowers were in full bloom. The yak-tails on the prows of the boats flapped in the breeze. People had heard about the capture of a famous Persian warrior and had come out of the walled city and gathered near the shore. A sea monster with glowing yellow scales and pointed teeth came out of the waters. After all, it was not every day that one got to see a fearless nobleman chained like a common criminal. Hamza's face was grey and weary, his hair matted. He thought, "What will happen to me now? How will I be able to escape?"

The giant Zumurrud Shah also came to see his feared enemy, and grunted in satisfaction when he saw the defeated Hamza bound in chains. Shahrashob grabbed Hamza by the shoulders, pulled him out of the boat, and threw him down before Malik Argus and Zumurrud Shah. "Bow down before me," roared Zumurrud Shah. But Hamza staggered to his feet. "I am a nobleman, the head of all the armies in Persia. I will only bow before God," he said. Zumurrud Shah was enraged at Hamza's boldness and unsheathed his sword to attack him. But Malik Argus stopped him, and shouted, "Don't kill Hamza! We will throw him into prison and let him suffer there. The great Amir's army will never be able to save him now."

The Walk to Prison

The storyteller shakes his head sadly; his voice is low and heavy: "Look, my friends—see what they have done to the great Amir..."

Amir Hamza, the great warrior, the hero of Persia, was paraded through the streets of Takaw like an animal. He was bound and chained to two armed guards. Three thousand soldiers marched on either side. Their decorated shields clanged as they marched and their long, curved swords were unsheathed and ready for action. Like a true nobleman, Hamza walked with his head held high, through the star-tiled city gates.

The road to the prison went past the caravanserai where Ayjil, Alamshah and Tul Mast lived. When they heard the heavy thud of marching feet, the three men looked out of the window and saw that their beloved leader was surrounded by Argus's soldiers. They bravely resolved to rescue their master. Together they vowed, "We will free our Amir—at any cost!"

Hamza was taken to an underground prison protected by a massive domed mountain. Heavily armed soldiers and Tamat, a seven-headed monster with the powerful body of a bear, guarded the prison. An enormous rock blocked the entrance to the dungeon. This rock needed 400 men to move it, and when moved, the thunderous noise boomed across the land, making people many miles away shudder with fright.

When Hamza arrived at the prison gates, Argus's guards tried to remove the huge rock and open

the dungeon gates. They heaved and strained, but the rock did not move. Then Hamza came forward and gave it one powerful kick. The rock rolled away and the entrance to the underground dungeon opened. The guards were astonished! How could one man's strength be more than that of 400 men? The soldiers bowed their heads with respect to the Amir but they had no choice except to obey their king's orders. A rope was tied around Hamza's waist and he was slowly lowered into the dark dungeon.

At first Hamza could see nothing. Then, as his eyes got used to the darkness, he saw a shadowy figure of another man sitting on the ground. Hamza called out, "Who are you?"
"I am Khushraw, son of King Jamshed, the rightful ruler of Takaw," the pale young man replied. "The evil Argus and his friend Zumurrud Shah killed my father and threw me into prison."
"How long have you been down here?"
"Twelve years."
Hamza was filled with rage at Malik Argus and Zumurrud Shah. He grasped the man's hand. "I will free you from the clutches of Argus and make you king," he promised.

Back in the caravanserai, Alamshah, Ayjil and Tul Mast were longing to meet their leader. They wanted to rush to the prison and set him free. But Ayjil was cautious. "There are hundreds of enemy soldiers guarding Hamza," he warned. "If we want to save Hamza, we will need help."

To fight Argus's army, Alamshah, Ayjil and Tul Mast decided they needed one of their own. They wrote a letter to the captain of Hamza's army. "The Amir is in danger. Bring your men and weapons to rescue him." Yunus, their boatman, was a trustworthy man and would carry the message to the captain in Sabayil. Yunus tucked the important letter into his belt and immediately set sail for Sabayil.

Umar Lost at Sea

The waves in the painting rise and fall but Yunus sails his boat with skill. "In a stormy sea a boat can capsize very easily," warns Darbar Khan.

Yunus the boatman had to get to Sabayil as quickly as possible to get help for Hamza. He rowed hard against angry waves. One evening, he saw a boat with a red and blue sail tossing in the sea alongside him. Yunus shouted with delight when he recognized the boat. It belonged to Hamza's loyal friend Umar, and the captain of Umar's boat was Yunus's brother. They had been lost at sea for many months and were relieved to meet Yunus.

"How do I know they were brothers?" asks the storyteller with a smile. "Look, their names are written in Persian on their sleeves."

Yunus and Umar exchanged news. When Umar heard about Hamza's capture, he asked for directions to Takaw. "Steer our boat towards Takaw right away," he directed his captain, "We must go and rescue our Amir." "Don't waste any time," he told Yunus. "You go to Sabayil and return with Hamza's army. I will wait for you in Takaw."

However, Takaw was still a long way off, and one afternoon after many days at sea, one of Umar's sailors climbed up the boat's tall mast to see what lay ahead. "Watch out!" he called, "There is a huge rocky mountain in front of us." As they sailed closer, Umar could see the densely wooded seashore and a shepherd watching over his goats. Suddenly the sailor shouted, from the top of the mast, "I see some towers. It looks like a citadel. Oh no! Perhaps we have arrived at the fortress of Mikhal the Champion." The sailors became very nervous when they discovered where they were, and wanted

to turn around immediately. Mikhal was known to chop off the heads of those who entered his fort. But Umar instructed his men to anchor the boat and he bravely walked up to the fort.

Mikhal the Champion was waiting at the gates. Umar looked him straight in the eye. “My lord and friend Amir Hamza has been captured by Malik Argus and Zumurrud Shah and is in great danger. Will your armies help us to rescue him?” he asked. Mikhal replied, “Last night I had a dream that the Amir’s friend would come to my fortress. I have been waiting for you, Umar. I have long admired Amir Hamza. I will bring my soldiers to Takaw by land, and we will soon free your Amir from those scoundrels.”

A Dangerous Mission

Emperor Akbar and the courtiers wait anxiously for the storyteller to continue his story. The air is so still that the forest itself seems to be holding its breath, wondering what will happen next. Akbar knows it will not be easy for Hamza's friends to rescue him from the prison. Darbar Khan turns a dark and frightening painting towards his audience, and starts to speak again...

After leaving Mikhal's fortress, Umar's boat finally arrived in Takaw and he strode directly to the caravanserai where he knew the three friends, Ayjil, Alamshah and Tul Mast were staying. Together they waited impatiently for Hamza's army from Persia and Mikhal the Champion to arrive.

There was no sign of the armies for several days and the men grew restless. They decided to take a walk to the prison where Hamza was trapped. At the gates, Tamat the seven-headed jailor stopped them. "What do you want?" he demanded harshly. "No visitors are allowed in this prison." The friends saluted him. Umar bowed low and presented him with a jewelled dagger. "We have heard that your prison is the safest in the world. They say that no man has ever escaped from the deep dungeons. How is that possible?" he asked.

Tamat's hairy chest puffed up with pride at this praise and he invited them to enter the prison." "Come, I will show you the massive rock that blocks the entrance to the dungeon. And do you know my clever way of checking on the prisoners? Three times a day, I lower a basket of food into the dark cell and when the basket comes up empty, I know that the prisoners are still there. Hamza and Khushraw have no chance of escape. They will die in that dungeon." He growled and showed his dirty yellow teeth.

The four men thanked Tamat for the tour of the prison and walked back dejectedly to the caravanserai. How would they rescue Hamza? Too many soldiers guarded the prison and the rock that blocked the entrance was as huge as a mountain. They sat on the dusty floor of their small room with their heads in their hands. Suddenly, Umar's face lit up with hope—he had thought of a plan. And with God's good grace, his plan would work.

On a moonless night, when the only lights they could see were the pinpricks of flashing fireflies, Hamza's friends wrapped themselves in sheets and crept along the alleys till they reached a quiet spot outside the prison walls. Armed with their shovels, they began to dig furiously, not stopping even to wipe the sweat off their tired faces. After an exhausting four hours, they had dug an underground tunnel to the dungeon where Hamza lay imprisoned. The first part of their plan to rescue Hamza was complete.

The four men inched their way forward, crawling like insects through the narrow passageway. Finally, they pushed the wall and fell exhausted and covered in mud, on to the floor of the dungeon. Hamza leapt up in surprise. "Praise the Lord!"

he shouted when he saw his friends. "How glad I am to see you! Quick! Remove my chains and the wooden board from my feet and unchain Khushraw. We must leave the cell before Tamat discovers that we have escaped."

While the others crawled out of the tunnel, Ayjil stayed behind and waited for Tamat the jailor to send down the basket of food. He took out the food and sent the empty basket up to Tamat. Tamat yawned loudly and settled down to take a nap. Then, as silently as a snake, Ayjil followed his friends through the tunnel. Now they were all outside the prison walls.

At last Hamza and Khushraw were free! But although they were out of the dungeon, they were not out of danger. When their escape was discovered, Tamat and his soldiers would certainly follow them. It was still dark outside, and the men quickly walked with Khushraw back to the safety of the caravanserai.

That same night, Malik Argus had the strangest nightmare. He dreamt that a seven-headed dragon had emerged from his jail. In his dream, the large, fire-breathing dragon bit off his throne, gobbled up his son, ate his entire kingdom and charged towards him with a terrible roar. Argus woke up sweating and frightened. He said to himself, "Is Hamza the dragon of my dreams? Will he throw me off my throne and kill my son?" He took the nightmare as a sign that a terrible calamity was about to take place. He dispatched his soldiers to the prison with orders to kill Hamza immediately.

But Argus's soldiers were too late! When the soldiers and Tamat entered the dungeon, Hamza and Khushraw had already escaped! Tamat and the soldiers crawled into the tunnel through which the prisoners had bolted. When they reached the end of the tunnel, outside the prison walls, Hamza and his four faithful friends were waiting for them. They attacked Argus's soldiers with heavy clubs, bound them in chains and threw them back into Tamat's prison.

Victory in Takaw

The last painting is taken out just as the moon begins to rise. Silvery moonbeams spread in the forest—but the painting Darbar Khan holds up is grim and dark. Akbar's soldiers shudder with fright when they see it.

The people of Takaw trembled when they saw Argus's chained soldiers and heard Amir Hamza, the world conqueror, shout: "I will send Malik Argus to hell and I will return the kingdom of Takaw to its rightful ruler, King Khushraw."

Hamza was fearless. He could fight eleven soldiers single-handedly and defeat them. When the people in Takaw saw his courage, they stood on the rooftops and cheered, "Victory to Amir Hamza! Long live King Khushraw!" Umar dragged Tamat the jailor out on the streets and commanded, "Bow down before my leader, Amir Hamza, you rotten scoundrel." When Tamat refused, Umar pulled out his sword and chopped off Tamat's nose. Everyone gasped in horror.

King Argus panicked when he heard that Tamat's nose had been hacked off. He rushed to Zumurrud Shah for advice. "What shall we do?" he asked, "No one is brave enough to fight Hamza." But the giant was not worried. "We have 50,000 men," he told Argus, "and Hamza has only his four friends. Ring a bell through the city and ask our men to take up arms and attack Hamza. He will soon be defeated."

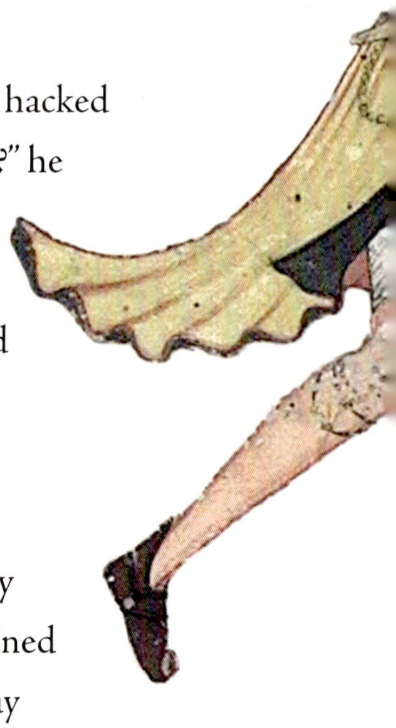

What Zumurrud Shah didn't realize was that Hamza's own army from Persia had already reached the shores of Takaw, and had joined forces with that of Mikhal the Champion. They were on their way to the city. A fierce and bloody battle was fought in the streets and the forces of Malik Argus and Zumurrud Shah were totally defeated. The people of Takaw rejoiced for the wicked rule of Argus and Zumurrud Shah had ended. Prince Khushraw became the new King of Takaw and like his father, Jamshed, he was a good and kind ruler.

As the moon begins to rise in the starry sky, Emperor Akbar embraces the old storyteller and presents him with a bag of gold coins. "My wise friend," he says, "you have taught us much today. If a man is brave and good, he can conquer anything—iron chains, dungeons and even seven-headed monsters. Come, my men," he calls to his soldiers, "Let us thank Darbar Khan."

Darbar Khan bows low as the soldiers cheer and clap. "Wait," he says as he holds up his hand. "The sun has set, and this part of my tale has ended. But Amir Hamza's adventures are not over. He must set sail once more across the dangerous seas, to Sabayil where his beautiful princess awaits him... and who knows what evil monsters and giants he will meet on the way?"

که اورا قدرت استنباط نباشد اصلا اما چون وصیتها صاحب صناعت
دران باب حفظ کند و تبانی بتتبع آن وصایا میکند عمل تام شود

Akbar's Painting Workshop

The *Hamzanama* was the most important project of Akbar's painting studio. In this manuscript there were 360 adventures, inscribed in calligraphy on gold-flecked pages. These stories were illustrated with 1400 magical pictures. The 14 volumes of the manuscript were kept in large wooden boxes in the *Kitab Khana* or the Royal Library and taken out when the emperor wished to hear about one of Hamza's adventures. Akbar had a deep interest in painting and closely examined the work of the artists in his workshop.

Who were the artists and where did they work?

The two chief artists of Akbar's studio had come from Persia with Akbar's father Humayun, and the others were mostly Hindu and Muslim painters from different regions in India.

The artists worked in a room of the *Kitab Khana*. Their main work at this time was illustrating manuscripts. They sat on the floor and three or four of them often worked together on one painting. A master artist would plan the design of the whole picture. Some artists specialized in battle scenes, others in facial expressions, landscapes or animals. Every week, the completed works were presented to Akbar and he would reward his painters with gold coins and jewels.

What materials did they use?

Akbar provided his artists with very good materials. The *Hamzanama* pictures were usually painted on paper glued to stiff cotton fabric and measured about two by two feet.

The brilliant colours in the *Hamzanama* paintings look as good as new today even though they were created nearly 450 years ago. The colours used in the paintings were made from different materials: plants, metals, stones and, sometimes, even insects. The artists made their own paints. First they crushed the materials to a fine powder with a heavy instrument. Then they a made a paste by adding the powdered colours to Gum Arabica, a glue made from the bark of a tree. The painters mixed their colours in the smooth white lining of clamshells. The paint brushes were made of squirrel, rabbit and other animal hair. Sometimes a brush with only a single hair would be used for painting fine and delicate lines.

Mughal Colour Palette

Vermillion is a rich red and came from the poisonous mineral cinnabar.

The man's *jama* is vermillion.

Crimson was made from crushed kermes insects. Crimson was also called lac because a lac (100,000) insects were needed to make the pigment.

This was used to paint Ashqar's shiny crimson coat.

Gold and silver were made from powdered precious metals. These were reserved for special parts of the painting only.

Here the artist has used this precious pigment to colour the shiny weapon.

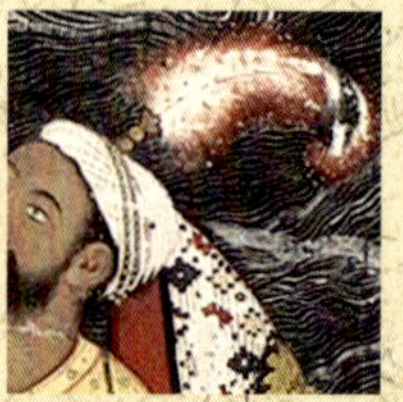

White was made from lead.

Look at the feathered turban and plume.

Green was made by mixing copper with salt water.

Here the blanket is painted green.

Orange was made by powdering red lead or *sindoor*. *Sindoor* is sacred to Hindus and used in religious ceremonies.

See how the artist has used this pigment on the *chinar* leaves.

Azure blue came from lapis lazuli. *Lapis* means stone and *azul* means blue. It is a rare and expensive mineral and is used in making jewellery.

The designs on the enamelled shield have been painted with this colour.

Dark blue was extracted from the indigo plant. It was called indigo because the plant originally came from India. Another name for it is *neel*—the Indian word for blue.

The waves were painted using this colour.

Black was made from soot.

This was used to paint the man's beard.

Bright yellow or *peori* was made from the bright yellow urine of cows fed on mango leaves.

The man's *jama* is painted with *peori*.

Ways of Seeing

BE AN ART DETECTIVE

Every painting tells us a story. This painting is an ancient Mughal painting. It tells us another tale from the *Hamzanama* and is almost 500 years old. There are no rules on how to look at a painting. You can start from the top or bottom, from the centre or from the sides. The main idea is to slow down your eyes and look carefully.

CAN YOU FIND THE STORY IN THIS PAINTING?

5 clues

Clue 1: Important people are often drawn larger or put in a place where they can be easily seen.

WHO are the main characters?

Look for the heroes in the story. On the left of the painting, stands the handsome warrior Hamza. Notice his weapons and his magical horse; Ashqar with the three eyes. Hamza's friend Umar has an axe in his hand and a dagger at his waist. The large soldier Madi stands guard at the bottom of the painting.

Clue 2: Actions of people tell you what is happening in the story.

WHAT are the men in the painting doing?

Hamza and his army arrive at a fortress. Zumurrud Shah, the evil giant and his army are hiding in the fortress. The drawbridge is nearly shut. Hamza's soldiers sound the battle drums. Will the enemy come out and fight? What shows us that the soldiers are ready for battle?

Clue 3: The setting of the story helps you to imagine where the action took place.

WHERE is the story happening?

The fortress is near an angry swollen river and is surrounded by huge slippery rocks. Does this look like any place you have been to?

Clue 4: The colours, the movement of people, and the expressions on their faces, together make up the mood of the painting.

HOW has the artist made us feel the mood of the story?

Hamza climbs a huge rock to look at the fortress. Umar runs excitedly towards him. The soldiers look ready for battle. Madi's face has a serious expression. Does this painting make you feel excited, frightened, happy or sad? Why?

Clue 5: The clothes the men wear and the weapons they carry tell us when the story took place.

WHEN did the story happen?

What tells us that the story took place a long time ago? Notice the dress and the weapons of the soldiers. In what way are today's battles different?

Illustration Credits

Page 4: Akbar crossing the Ganga in 1567, *Akbarnama* circa 1590, Victoria and Albert Museum, London

Page 12: Akbar hunts near Lahore and Hamid Bakari is punished by having his head shaved and having him mounted on an ass, *Akbarnama* circa 1590, Victoria and Albert Museum, London

Page 15: Shahrashob seizes the Amir and puts him in a boat, *Hamzanama* circa 1570, MAK—Austrian Museum of Applied Arts/Contemporary Art, Vienna

Page 20: Umar boards a ship and goes in search of the Amir, *Hamzanama* circa 1570, MAK—Austrian Museum of Applied Arts/Contemporary Art, Vienna

Page 23: Ayjil, Alamshah and Tul Zangi are recognized by Khwaja Nu'man in the city of Takaw, *Hamzanama* circa 1570, MAK—Austrian Museum of Applied Arts/Contemporary Art, Vienna

Page 28: Mahlaj displays his skills before Zumurrud Shah, *Hamzanama* circa 1570, MAK—Austrian Museum of Applied Arts/Contemporary Art, Vienna

Page 31: Shahrashob reaches Takaw, *Hamzanama* circa 1570, MAK—Austrian Museum of Applied Arts/Contemporary Art, Vienna

Page 35: Shahrashob leads Hamza to prison, *Hamzanama* circa 1570, MAK—Austrian Museum of Applied Arts/Contemporary Art, Vienna

Page 39: Hamza's friends send Yunus the sailor for help, *Hamzanama* circa 1570, MAK—Austrian Museum of Applied Arts/Contemporary Art, Vienna

Page 42: After the arrival of Umar, the three friends dig a tunnel and free Hamza, *Hamzanama* circa 1570, MAK—Austrian Museum of Applied Arts/Contemporary Art, Vienna

Page 46: During a fight in the caravanserai, Umar takes a dagger and cuts off Shahrashob's nose, *Hamzanama* circa 1570, MAK—Austrian Museum of Applied Arts/Contemporary Art, Vienna

Page 48: The *Kitab Khana, The Akhlaq-I-Nasiri* (*Kitab Khana*) attributed to Sajnu, AKTC 2005.1.288. [MS93 fol.95] © Aga Khan Trust for Culture, formerly in the collection of Prince and Princess Sadruddin Aga Khan

Page 52: The Amir, Umar and Umar Ma'dikarb arrive at Noshad Pass, *Hamzanama* circa 1570, MAK—Austrian Museum of Applied Arts/Contemporary Art, Vienna

Bibliography

Berinstain, Valerie. *Mughal India: Splendours of the Peacock Throne*. London: Thames and Hudson Ltd., 1998.

Eraly, Abraham. *Emperors of the Peacock Throne: The Saga of the Great Moghuls*. India: Penguin Books India, 2001.

Faridany-Akhavan, Zahra. "All the King's Toys." *Muqarnas: An Annual on Islamic Art and Architecture*, Volume X (1993): 292–298.

Galbi, Douglas."Hamzanama of Akbar: A Masterpiece of Art from the Islamic World." http://www.galbithink.org/sense-s3.htm

Gascoigne, Bamber. *The Great Moguls*. London: Jonathan Cape, 1971.

Schimmel, Annemarie. *The Empire of the Great Mughals: History, Art and Culture*. India: Oxford University Press, 2005.

Seyller, John, Ebba Koch and Rainald Franz. *The Adventures of Hamza: Painting and Storytelling in Mughal India*. Washington, D. C.: Freer Gallery of Art and Arthur M. Sackler Gallery, Smithsonian Institution, 2002.

Stronge, Susan. *Painting for the Mughal Emperor: The Art of the Book 1560–1660*. London: Victoria and Albert Museum, 2002.

Further Reading and Information for Children

To see more paintings from the *Hamzanama*
The Smithsonian Museum's online exhibition:
http://www.asia.si.edu/exhibitions/online/hamza/default.htm
http://www.asia.si.edu/press/hamzathumbnails.pdf

To learn more about Mughal India
The British Museum's interactive website:
http://www.mughalindia.co.uk/room.html

To learn more about art in South and South-east Asia
The Asia Society's educational website:
http://www.askasia.org/
The Metropolitan Museum's website:
http://www.metmuseum.org/explore/publications/asia.htm
The San Diego Museum of Art's exploration of the art of the Great Mughals:
http://www.sdmart.org/exhibition-binney-mughals.html

To learn about how the *Hamzanama* paintings were acquired by the Victoria and Albert Museum:
http://www.vam.ac.uk/collections/asia/object_stories/hamzanama/index.html

Acknowledgements

We would like to thank:

Professor John Seyller, whose amazing catalogue produced to accompany the exhibition "The Adventures of Hamza" organized by the Arthur M. Sackler Gallery, Smithsonian Institution, Washington, D. C., was the cornerstone of this project.

Dr. Milo Cleveland Beach, for his encouragement, advice and for writing the foreword to this book.

Anita Roy, for editing the book and making the words sing.

Thomas Matyk, MAK Museum, Vienna, who along with the permissions for the incredible paintings used in this book, gave us great support.

The Aga Khan Trust for Culture, for the use of the miniature *The Akhlaq-I-Nasiri* (*Kitab Khana*) attributed to Sajnu-Fol.95 MS 39.

Dr. Wheeler Thackston and Zareen Hodiwalla for help with the translations.

Dr. Eberhard Fischer, Dr. B. N. Goswamy, Radhika & Hans Hertzberger, Lisa Heydlauff, Varsha Bajaj, Neeta Premchand and Vinay Chowdhry for their valuable advice.

Aurobind Patel and Chelna Desai for their creative input on the design of the book.

Nira and Shyam Benegal, who helped us take the first big step.

Our friends, relatives and colleagues who patiently heard the many changing versions of the Hamzanama, gave us their ideas, made critical comments and urged us to go on.

We would also like to thank:

MDM:
My husband, Aditya Mangaldas, and my daughters, Ayesha and Amaya, for allowing me to have my own adventure in search of Hamza and putting up with all my idiosyncrasies. My family, Shreya and Kishore Dalal, Sunil and Mamta Dalal, Nirmala and Rasiklal Maneklal, Devi Mangaldas and Aditi Mangaldas, for encouraging me to reach for the stars.

SM:
My husband, Mehli, for quietly encouraging me to go further and always believing that the book would be successfully completed. Shaheen and Rishad, one a muse and an inspiration, the other a critic and a creative flow that spilled over. Both unwavering in their belief that the story would be well-told.

This edition published in 2010 by
Mapin Publishing Pvt. Ltd
502 Paritosh, Near Darpana Academy
Usmanpura Riverside
Ahmedabad 380013 INDIA
T: 91 79 402 28 228 | F: 91 79 402 28 201
E: mapin@mapinpub.com | www.mapinpub.com

Simultaneously published in the
United States of America in 2010 by
Grantha Corporation
77 Daniele Drive, Hidden Meadows
Ocean Township, NJ 07712
E: mapin@mapinpub.com

ISBN: 978-81-88204-84-7 (Mapin)
ISBN: 978-0-944142-86-8 (Grantha)
LCCN: 2010923268

First published in India in 2007 by
Mapin Publishing
in association with
HarperCollins *Children's* Books, an imprint of
HarperCollins *Publishers* India

Typeset in Adobe Jenson Pro, CalligraphBT
Designed by Bhavika Shah / Mapin Design Studio
Edited by Anita Roy
Copyedited by Ayesha Kagal

Printed and bound at Thomson Press, India

Not for sale in the Indian sub-continent